The Meat-Eating Plants Next Door

Written by Sarah Glasscock

Illustrated by Judy Love

STECK-VAUGHN

A Harcourt Company

www.steck-vaughn.com

Contents

Almost immediately after the moving van left the Chens' new house, the doorbell rang. Diana answered the door to find an older woman holding a platter of sandwiches.

"Welcome to the neighborhood," the woman said. "I'm Mary Bell, your next-door neighbor on that side." She pointed to her right with her head. "Are you hungry?"

Diana was *starving*. She swallowed and nodded.

Before Diana could introduce herself, Mary Bell handed the platter to her. "Good. I'll be back with more food and some lemonade." As Mary Bell hurried down the porch steps, her long gray braid swayed.

Kelsey, Diana's older sister, walked into the living room, sniffing. "I smell turkey—and I don't mean you." She took a sandwich and wandered upstairs without even asking where they had come from.

"You're welcome!" Diana yelled after Kelsey.

The doorbell rang. Carefully balancing the platter, Diana opened the door. A girl her own age stood on the porch.

"You're not Mary Bell!" she said in surprise.

"Nope, I'm Carrie Jackson," the girl answered. "I live around the corner. We moved here last month."

Diana was about to shake Carrie's outstretched hand, but Carrie was reaching for a sandwich. "Help yourself," Diana told her.

"Thanks." Carrie took a huge bite of the sandwich and chewed. "Yum. Tomato and cheese. You really should put that platter down somewhere and try one."

Looking helplessly around the empty room, Diana wondered if Carrie offered advice to people all the time. "You don't happen to play softball, do you?" she asked Carrie.

"I *love* softball!" Carrie exclaimed. "But please tell me you're not a catcher." She grabbed a sandwich and held it up to Diana's mouth. "Here, take a bite."

Armed with a pitcher of lemonade, a bowl of salad, and a plate of brownies, Mary Bell entered the front door. "Here's the rest of lunch," she said cheerfully.

"Hey, everybody!" Carrie shouted. "LUNCH!"

Hearing a strange voice, Diana's parents hurried into the living room. As Diana introduced them to Mary Bell and Carrie—and Mary and Carrie to each other—Diana thought, "I think I might like living here."

Soon Diana and Carrie were practicing softball almost every afternoon. When they played in Diana's backyard, Mary Bell was usually in her backyard. Instead of a lawn, Mary's backyard had a garden with tidy rows of vegetables, flowers, and herbs. Attached to the side of her house stood a greenhouse made of frosted glass.

One afternoon Carrie threw a wild pitch, and Diana knocked the ball into Mary's garden. "Mary!" Diana shouted. "Watch out!"

"DUCK!" Carrie yelled.

Instead of ducking, Mary bolted up, shot her arm out, and caught the ball. Then she rapidly fired it back to Carrie.

Carrie was so astonished by Mary's reaction that she stood rooted to the ground with her mouth open. Diana had to pull her out of the way of the softball.

"You're letting go of the ball too soon," Mary told Carrie and bent over to weed her tomato plants again.

"Well, I'm really a catcher, you know," Carrie called out to Mary.

Mary Bell stood back up and walked over to the low stone wall that separated her house from Diana's. "You still have to know how to throw the ball," she stated. "And knowing how to throw it means knowing when to release it. You let go of it too soon. That's why it went over Diana's head."

Carrie frowned and started to march over to the wall. "But I—"

Diana grabbed Carrie's arm. "Shh," she whispered. "How come you know so much about softball?" she asked Mary.

Standing up, Mary straightened her hat. "What you really mean is how come an old woman like me knows so much about softball."

Diana started to apologize, but Mary held up her hand to stop her. "It's all right," she said with a laugh. Then she motioned for Diana and Carrie to go to her front door. "I'll tell you about me and softball over some lemonade and cookies."

As Mary opened the front door of her house, Diana's eyes widened. Plants filled Mary's every room. Trees in huge clay pots filled the corners and the spaces in front of the windows.

Long runners of green and yellow leaves trailed down from pots perched on top of bookcases. African violets with soft, velvety leaves and tiny purple flowers nestled together on tables. Baskets of ferns hung from the ceilings. Pots full of bushy and feathery herbs lined the walls in her kitchen.

Mary encouraged Diana and Carrie to rub the leaves of the herbs and smell them. Then she cut some and placed them in plastic bags for Diana and Carrie to take home. "Plants are so interesting," Mary told them. "Have you ever seen a cactus burst into bloom after a rain?"

"I'll bet it's not as interesting as softball," Diana replied."

Mary smiled and said mysteriously, "You might be surprised. But I know you're more interested in softball than plants right now. Wait here." She disappeared into a hallway. Diana heard her opening doors and pulling out boxes in another room. Carrie was more interested in examining the cookies, which had tiny seeds in them.

When Mary finally returned, she carried a large photograph album. "I haven't looked at this in years," she told the girls with a sigh. She opened the album carefully, but little bits of photographs crumbled onto the kitchen table. She pointed to a picture. "I was about your age—ten—when this picture was taken. It was the city championship game. We won that game thirteen to eleven."

"Wow!" Diana breathed. "What position did you play?"

"First base. I tagged Emily Watts for the final out," Mary said. She couldn't hide the pride in her voice.

"So you weren't a catcher?" Carrie asked. "I didn't think so." She sniffed her cookie and took a small bite.

Mary turned the page. A small cloud of dust drifted into the air. "I started catching in high school and continued all through college."

The pictures that filled the pages showed Mary as a teenager, crouching to catch strikes and balls, whirling or jumping to capture foul balls, and tagging players out at home. The photos captured her batting, running like a whirlwind around the bases, and sliding into home.

As Diana studied the photographs, a plan began to form in her mind. "Maybe you could coach Carrie and me sometime," she suggested.

"I don't need any coaching," Carrie announced. She stood up. "I'd better go."

"Well, I sure could use some coaching for my hitting," Diana said as she reluctantly followed Carrie to the door.

"How about this—I'll help you with your hitting, and you can help me in my greenhouse," Mary suggested. "You're welcome to come, too, Carrie."

"We could start tomorrow afternoon!" Diana said excitedly. "Would that be all right?"

"I'm expecting a shipment of plants tomorrow. You must come over and see my new sundews, and then we'll practice." Mary held out the plastic bags. "Don't forget your herbs."

"Oh, *great*," Carrie mumbled under her breath as she took her bag.

"What's wrong with you?" Diana asked Carrie as soon as they left Mary's house.

"What's wrong with *me*?" Carrie shot back. "Nothing's wrong with *me*. Your neighbor's the one who's strange."

Chapter 2
What Does Carnivorous Mean?

The next morning, Diana called Carrie. "Guess what? My dad stuck a bunch of that thyme Mary gave us inside a chicken and then roasted it. It tasted great."

"Yuck!" Carrie said. "I threw mine in the trash can."

"Why did you do that?" Diana asked. She was totally puzzled by Carrie's behavior.

"How do you know Mary Bell wasn't trying to poison us?" Carrie questioned. "I mean, do you really feel all right after eating that stuff? How about the rest of your family—are they feeling okay?"

Diana was reconsidering whether or not she wanted to invite Carrie over to play softball. "We all thought the chicken tasted delicious. Even my sister." She thought about pretending to hear her mother calling her so that she could hang up.

"You know, Diana, I *can* throw a ball. I do *not* throw it over people's heads," Carrie insisted.

To Diana's relief, her mother actually did call her name.

"I have to go," Diana told Carrie. "My mom needs me. Bye." Hanging up before Carrie could say anything else, she went to see what her mother wanted.

Her mother was in the backyard, chatting with Mary Bell over the wall. She held an armful of lettuce and carrots. "Look what Mary's given us. We've got salad for tonight."

"My dad used your thyme in the chicken last night," Diana told Mary. "It tasted great."

Diana's mother tapped a carrot thoughtfully against her cheek. "You know, Mary, you've given us so much food that the least we can do is have you over for dinner. Are you free tomorrow evening?"

Mary beamed. "I am. What can I bring?"

"Bring your scrapbook with all the pictures of you playing softball," Diana said eagerly. "Kelsey didn't believe me when I told her you were a softball champion."

"I was on a championship softball team," Mary corrected. "You know it takes the entire team to win a game."

Diana didn't think Mary really meant to embarrass her, but she felt the tips of her ears grow warm anyway. "Right," she mumbled.

"By the way, Diana, Mary needs a favor. Would you mind watching for a delivery man when she goes out?" her mother asked.

"When I get back and get my new sundews all settled, we can practice throwing and batting," Mary said. "How does that sound?"

Diana nodded.

"Just make sure the delivery man puts the box of sundews in the shade on the porch," Mary told Diana. "I should be back by noon." She trotted to the front of her house and got into her car. As she backed out of her driveway, she waved.

Diana and her mother waved back. "Mom, what's a sundew?" Diana asked.

Her mother shrugged. "I'm not sure. It sounds like the name of a watermelon or something. Let's go look it up in the encyclopedia or on the Internet."

"I'll do it later," Diana said. "Maybe the delivery guy will know when he comes," she thought.

Her mother frowned. "Why not do it now?"

Luckily, the delivery van pulled up in front of Mary's house, and Diana didn't have to answer. Hopping over the wall, she ran to greet the delivery man, who eased a large box out of the back of the truck and placed it on a dolly. Then he wheeled the dolly to Mary Bell's front porch.

Diana followed him to the porch. "I'm Diana Chen from next door. Mary Bell asked me to tell you to put the box in the shade."

"Better not get too close, Diana Chen," the man said after he unloaded the box. "Better keep kittens, puppies, and small children away from this box, too."

CAUTION
LIVE
PLANTS

Diana couldn't tell if the man was joking, but she stepped backward cautiously. "Why should I do that?"

The man shook his finger at Diana. "Because sundews are carnivorous, that's why."

"They're what?" Diana asked.

"Carnivorous. You know what that means, don't you?" The man raised his eyebrows. "Good luck. I've got other deliveries." Then he left.

Diana placed her ear close to the cardboard box and thought she heard soft, scratching sounds inside it. She jumped away from the box and stared at it.

From her bedroom window, Kelsey shouted down at her sister. "What are you doing over there?"

"What does *carnivorous* mean?" Diana shouted back to Kelsey.

"Come home and look it up yourself," her sister answered and walked away from her window.

Diana was circling the box when Carrie rode by on her bicycle. "What are you doing with that box?" Carrie asked.

"Come here! It's the sundews. They're carnivorous," Diana answered. She figured Carrie might know what the word meant.

"GET AWAY FROM THAT BOX!" Carrie shrieked.

Carrie's response shocked Diana so much that she almost tumbled off the porch. Then Carrie practically dragged her to the sidewalk. "Do you want to get your fingers bitten off?" she asked.

"What are you talking about?" Diana asked.

"The word *carnivorous* means 'meat-eating,'" Carrie informed her. "That box is filled with meat-eating plants!"

Just then Mary Bell pulled into her driveway and honked her horn. Diana and Carrie stared at her and then ran as fast as they could to Carrie's house. They threw themselves underneath an oak tree and tried to catch their breath.

"Her whole greenhouse is probably filled with meat-eating plants. And she wanted us to help her in her greenhouse in exchange for softball practice!" Carrie said. "She wanted to feed us to her plants!"

Diana stared at Carrie. "I don't think that's what she wanted to do."

"What happened to the people who used to live in your house?" Carrie demanded. "I'll bet you don't even know."

That evening Diana tiptoed out of the house and crawled along the wall near Mary Bell's greenhouse. Although she couldn't see through the wavy glass, she could observe Mary Bell's shadow and the ragged shadows of plants against the glass wall. She could also hear Mary Bell's voice.

"Open wide, my little sundew. I have a nice bit of meat for you. Pitcher plant, I have a treat for you, too."

Chapter 3
Why Do You Think It's Called a Cobra Plant?

The next morning, Diana called Carrie to come over to her house. When Carrie arrived, Diana was in her bedroom, looking at Mary's house through a pair of binoculars. "I saw her feeding her plants in the greenhouse last night," Diana told Carrie with a shudder. "She *talks* to them while she feeds them!"

Carrie grabbed Diana's shoulder. "There she is!"

The two girls watched as Mary Bell went into her backyard. She was carrying a glass jar and a small net in one hand and a wire cage in the other. Tucking the net under one arm, Mary set the cage down between two rows of plants in her garden. She pulled up a few baby carrots and heads of lettuce and placed them in the bottom of the cage. Then Mary propped open the cage door. When she stuck the handle of the net into the trap, the trap door fell down with a snap.

Satisfied, Mary propped open the door again and began waving the net in the air.

"What's she doing?" Carrie whispered.

Mary cupped the open end of the net with her hand and then shook the contents of the net into the glass jar.

"She's catching flies for her plants," Diana whispered back.

Suddenly Mary looked up and waved at them. "Yoo-hoo! Why don't you two come over? We can play a little softball, and then I'll show you my new sundews!"

Diana slammed the window shut. She and Carrie ran downstairs to the kitchen where her parents were making bread.

"What's wrong with you two? You look like you've seen a monster," her father joked.

"We *have*," Carrie said.

"So, Dad, who lived in this house before us?" Diana asked. "What happened to them?"

He scratched his head and left a smudge of flour in his dark hair. "Let's see—I think somebody said they just disappeared in the middle of the night."

Diana's mother threw flour in his direction. "Your father's joking. Mary Bell said they were very nice people. They moved to Colorado. Carrie, didn't you know them? The Simpsons?"

"No," Carrie muttered. "They must have been eaten—I mean *moved away*—before we moved here."

Diana's mother looked closely at Diana and Carrie. "What's going on? What are you two up to?"

"We're not up to anything," Diana protested.

"But we know somebody who is," Carrie added.

"Dad, what's a sundew?" Diana asked.

He scratched his head again and left a second streak of flour in his hair. "I don't know. Is it some kind of soft drink?"

Diana's mother smiled. "I know what a sundew is because I looked it up in the encyclopedia."

"I know what a sundew is, too," said Carrie. "A sundew is a plant—a MEAT-EATING plant."

"That's right," Diana's mother agreed. "They usually eat flies and other kinds of insects."

Smacking his lips, Diana's father said, "Flies—yum!"

Diana and Carrie stared at him. "It's not funny, Dad," Diana said. "Insects aren't the only thing sundews eat."

The timer on the stove rang. Diana's mother pulled out two loaves of bread with rounded brown tops. "Then you did look up information about sundews, Diana. That's good!"

Diana shook her head. "No, I was spying on Mary Bell, and I saw her feeding pieces of—"

"Stop right there, Diana. I don't want you spying on Mary Bell or anyone else," her father stated.

"But, Dad," Diana protested. "She's—"

"I don't want to hear it," he said firmly. "I don't want you spying on anyone."

Diana's mother wrapped a loaf of bread in a blue-checked napkin. "I want you and Carrie to take this bread over to Mary. Tell her we're *all* looking forward to seeing her tonight for dinner. You're invited, too, Carrie."

Carrie gasped. "No way—I mean no, thank you."

22

Diana thought fast. "Actually, Carrie and her family invited me over for dinner tonight. They asked me last week, and I kind of already said yes."

"That's right," Carrie nodded. "We already bought a turkey and everything. My mom's polishing the silver, too. We're all *really* excited that Diana's coming over for dinner tonight."

Handing the wrapped loaf of bread to Diana, her mother said to her, "You're eating dinner here tonight. End of discussion. Now take this bread to Mary."

Diana and Carrie trudged over to Mary Bell's. Leaving the bread on her porch, they rang her doorbell—and ran.

Although Diana pulled the pillow tightly over her ears, she could still hear her mother calling her name. She had heard the doorbell ring, too. Mary Bell was downstairs.

Suddenly the pillow flew from Diana's hands. Kelsey rolled Diana over. "You'd better get downstairs. We've been waiting for you."

"Don't you think there's something weird about Mary Bell?" Diana asked.

"No, but I think there's something weird about you," Kelsey answered. "Just the other day, you were going on and on about how cool Mary was. Now you think she's weird. What happened?"

Shutting her eyes, Diana ignored her sister. She didn't want to look around her bedroom. The yellow walls seemed to soak up the sun during the day and shine softly at night. All her things were finally unpacked and arranged perfectly around the room. But when Diana looked out her window, she saw Mary Bell's house. It wasn't fair that she was living next door to a woman who grew meat-eating plants.

Kelsey nudged Diana's shoulder. "Mary brought a present for you. It's a plant."

Staring at her sister in horror, Diana whispered, "What kind of plant is it?"

"I think she called it a sundrop or a dewdrop or something like that." Kelsey shrugged. "It's cute. You'll like it."

Their father appeared in the doorway. "Girls," he said, "we're waiting downstairs for you."

Diana went downstairs unhappily. She would have to find a way to get rid of the plant before it got too hungry and started biting everyone.

Sitting on a table in the living room, the sundew glowed in the last rays of sunlight coming through the window. Diana moved closer to the plant. Tiny hairs covered its leaves, and a drop of something hung from the end of each hair.

"That's the glue that traps flies and other insects," Mary explained.

Diana backed away from the plant. "I don't feel very well," she told her parents. "I'd better go upstairs and lie down."

"Oh, that's too bad," Mary said.

Diana's father blocked her way. "You'll feel better after you've eaten something." He bent down and whispered, "I want you to behave, Diana."

Of course, her parents made her sit beside Mary. Kelsey got to sit across the table from them and tap Diana's knee with her foot. "Diana can't wait to practice softball with you," Kelsey said. "She couldn't stop talking about you the other night."

"Really?" Mary looked pleased.

"Actually, Carrie's father has offered to coach us," Diana lied.

"Oh, how nice," Mary said and tried to smile.

For the first time that night, Diana really looked at Mary. Bandages covered the woman's fingers, and her arms were scratched. "What happened to your arms and hands?" Diana asked.

"Oh, I'm fine. The bandages make it look worse than it really is," Mary answered.

"It looks pretty serious to me," Diana insisted. "It looks like something *attacked* you."

Mary laughed. "I got a little tangled in a plant that didn't want its branches trimmed. I should have worn my gloves."

"Sounds like your plants have feelings," Kelsey said.

Using a fork to push the peas around her plate, Diana thought about the sundew. Maybe she could accidentally knock it off the table and break its pot. Then she could throw the pot—and the sundew—away.

Before Diana knew it, dinner was over. "Diana can walk you home," she heard her mother tell Mary.

Diana bent over and groaned. "Oh, my stomach!"

Her mother led her into the kitchen. "I want you to stop pretending to be sick and walk Mary home."

On the way home, Mary Bell gripped Diana's arm as if her fingers were glued to Diana's sleeve. "There's no moon tonight. That's why it's so dark," she commented.

When Diana remained quiet, Mary continued, "I can't wait to show you my cobra plant. It's a big favorite with kids your age. The hood puffs up, and it really does look just like a cobra. It has fangs, too."

Diana jerked her arm out of Mary's grasp and ran home.

Chapter 4
What's In The Box?

That night Diana tossed and turned. She couldn't go to sleep, knowing that the sundew was downstairs . . . growing. Finally she slipped out of bed and carried the plant outside. Sneaking over the low wall, Diana crept through the rows of plants in Mary's garden. She was about to set down the sundew beside a sprawling squash plant when she heard the sound of an animal moving nearby. Surprised, Diana fell backward into two pepper plants.

After standing up and peeling the smashed peppers off her pajamas, Diana realized the animal was trapped in the cage Mary had put out. It was a small gray rabbit, and it was contentedly eating carrots and lettuce. Diana opened the cage door, but the rabbit didn't move. Finally she tilted the cage and shooed the rabbit out of it.

Then Mary's backyard light went on. For a second, Diana was blinded by the light.

"Who's out there? You'd better get going right now!"
Mary threatened. Diana ran for her life.

Carrie's eyes grew wide as she listened to Diana's
story. "Then what happened?"

"Mary called the police," Diana revealed. "I sneaked
back inside and got into bed and pretended to sleep
through the whole thing."

Tiptoeing to the window, Carrie pulled the curtains
apart and peered out. "Wow, you really flattened those
pepper plants."

"Do you see her?" Diana asked.

"Nope. Wait—here she comes. She's shaking the carrot tops out of the trap. I can't believe she was going to feed a *rabbit* to those nasty plants of hers."

During the night, Diana had come up with a plan. Everybody thought Mary Bell was a nice woman. Without some kind of proof, nobody was going to believe that she and her plants were dangerous. Diana and Carrie were going to follow Mary around until they got the proof they needed.

"My cousin says that plants have feelings," Carrie told Diana. "Maybe Mary Bell's plants are *making* her do what they want. Maybe they want to move into your house. Maybe they want to take over the world. That could be why Mary Bell gave that plant to you."

Diana swallowed hard. "Then we'd better get to work. Don't forget to bring your camera when you come over tonight."

That night Diana and Carrie took turns watching Mary's house and sleeping. At six in the morning, Diana shook Carrie awake. "She's up!" Diana hissed.

Carrie stumbled to the window after Diana. They watched as Mary walked through her garden and examined her plants. Then she placed her right leg on the low wall and stretched. She did the same thing with her left leg. Before Diana and Carrie could get dressed, Mary hopped on top of the wall, walked to the front sidewalk, and disappeared.

The girls scrambled to catch up to her. They darted behind bushes and cut through neighbors' yards—except for those with dogs they didn't know—to keep Mary in sight. Finally Mary jogged back to her house. They could hear her singing in the kitchen as she cooked breakfast.

Diana sniffed the air. "Do you smell that bacon? I'm starving."

"Yeah, but is it for her or her plants?" Carrie asked.

They just had time to sneak back into Diana's house for breakfast before anyone missed them.

"What are you girls going to do today?" Diana's mother asked.

Through the kitchen window, Diana spotted Mary walking out her front door. She was carrying an armful of library books. Several letters stuck out of one of the books.

Diana plunked her glass of orange juice on the table. "I totally forgot! My library books are due today! I have to take them back *right now*!" She grabbed Carrie's hand and rushed out the door.

At the library, they hid behind the bookshelves as Mary wandered up and down the rows of books.

"She's moving all over the place," Diana said. "So far, she's been in the fiction section, the gardening section, the biography section, and the magazine section. That's really weird."

"Yeah, it's like she's interested in *everything*," Carrie agreed.

They followed Mary to the post office, where she mailed letters and bought stamps. After that, Mary walked around different neighborhoods. In front of certain houses, she pulled out a small notebook and wrote in it. Then Mary had lunch with two friends.

Wearing sunglasses, Diana and Carrie hid behind menus and whispered to each other. The waitress was about to ask them to order or leave when Mary finished her lunch. Diana and Carrie hurried after her.

They hurried, that is, until Mary walked into the hospital. "I'm not going in there," Carrie declared.

It seemed as if Mary stayed inside for hours and hours, but she finally reappeared. She was carrying a large cardboard box.

"I wonder what's in the box," Diana said slowly.

"I don't think I want to know," Carrie replied. "But I'll bet her plants have a *really* good meal tonight."

After returning home, Mary spent the rest of the afternoon working in her garden. Then she cooked dinner, washed her dishes, and disappeared into her greenhouse. Diana and Carrie were exhausted and fell asleep before Mary Bell did.

"We still don't have any proof," Diana said the next day. "I wish we could see what's in that box she brought home from the hospital."

Carrie took a deep breath. "Okay, tomorrow when Mary goes for a walk, go with her. I'll sneak in the greenhouse."

Diana thought Carrie's idea might be against the law. But the next morning, at five forty-five, she was in front of Mary's house. Carrie waited in the bushes beside the porch. They waited and they waited.

"Maybe we missed her," Carrie whispered.

Diana shook her head. "No, she always leaves the house at exactly six o'clock."

By lunchtime, there was still no sign of Mary Bell. Diana couldn't stand it anymore, so she stood on her toes and peered into one of Mary's windows. "Oh, no!" she gasped.

Diana dashed to her house with Carrie hot on her heels. "What happened?" Carrie asked. "What did you see in there?"

"Hey, what's the rush?" Diana's father asked when the girls barreled into the kitchen.

"Something's happened to Mary!" Diana blurted out. "She's lying on her living room floor. A ladder's on top of her!"

Her father called 911 and then hurried over to Mary's house. When he turned the doorknob, the front door opened. "Wait out here," he told the girls.

Soon an ambulance and a fire truck with sirens blaring pulled up in front of Mary's house. Men and women hurried inside. In a few minutes, they brought Mary out on a stretcher. She smiled weakly when she saw the girls. "Thank you for saving me," she told them. Then she was whisked into the ambulance.

"What happened, Dad?" Diana asked. "Was it the plants?"

He thought for a second. "In a way, I guess it was. Mary was standing on the ladder to hang a plant, and she lost her balance. Her leg is severely broken, but she's going to be okay."

Diana and Carrie looked through the open door into Mary's living room. Then they looked at each other. Now was their chance.

Diana's father studied Diana and Carrie. "It's good that you found Mary today, but this spying thing has to stop." Then he closed the front door and locked it. "I'm going to buy snow cones for you two heroes. Let's go."

Mary had to stay in the hospital for almost a week. Diana's parents took turns caring for her plants. Diana and Carrie watched Diana's parents for any signs of change. They were afraid the plants might start controlling them. "They seem all right, don't they?" Diana asked Kelsey every time their parents returned from Mary's.

Kelsey always said the same thing. "They're parents. Sometimes it's hard to tell whether they're all right." Then Mary was released from the hospital, and something really terrible happened.

Diana looked at her mother in shock. "*What*?"

"I said you'd be glad to help Mary until her leg heals," her mother repeated. "You can start by taking this tray of food over for her lunch. There's enough for you, too." She wouldn't even give Diana time to call Carrie and reveal what was happening. *The plants have gotten to my mom,* Diana said to herself. Taking tiny steps, she walked to Mary's.

"Come on in! The door's open," Mary called. She lay on a sofa in the living room. Her leg was wrapped in a cast up to her knee. A pair of crutches lay across a nearby chair.

As Diana slowly entered the room, she saw that Mary's house had even more plants than before. One plant had thick silver leaves that curled back, and a bright pink flower rose from the middle of the leaves. Another plant had a long stem that ended in a yellow flower with brown speckles.

"Aren't they beautiful?" Mary asked.

Diana gazed around the room. All around her shone hundreds of leaves and bright flowers. To her surprise, she found herself nodding in agreement.

"I asked your parents to bring some of my plants from the greenhouse into the living room so I could see them," Mary said.

After they had eaten lunch, Mary stood up on her crutches. "Let's go into the greenhouse," she said.

Diana thought for a moment and realized she was curious about the greenhouse, but in a good way. She wanted to see more of Mary's plants.

The air inside the greenhouse smelled earthy and felt steamy. Diana stopped beside a vine that climbed up a post. It had long leaves and several long, thin stems. The end of each stem held something that looked like a container. "What's this called?" she asked.

"That's a pitcher plant. It comes from Asia. Do you see the pitchers growing on the stems?" Mary carefully opened a jar, and a fly flew into one of the pitchers. "It's a carnivorous plant."

Carrie burst through the door of the greenhouse, almost upsetting a tray of plants. "STOP! I know what *carnivorous* means! Don't you dare feed my friend to your plants!"

Although Diana was impressed by how brave Carrie was, she was also angry that her friend had almost trampled several plants.

Mary laughed. "Girls, I think we need to have a little talk. The word *carnivorous* does mean 'meat-eating,' but carnivorous plants eat insects. If I really tried to feed them other kinds of meat, they'd die."

"I knew that," Carrie mumbled.

"You did not!" Diana said.

Mary continued. "Now, I know I sometimes say things that hurt people's feelings. For instance, I once made someone who was actually a very good catcher feel like she wasn't very good. I'm sorry about that."

Diana's face grew red as she thought about how she and Carrie had let their imaginations run wild about Mary and her plants. "We're sorry about following you and thinking . . . what we were thinking," she told Mary.

"It's a good thing you did follow me, or I might still be lying on my living room floor," Mary said. "Why don't we start over?"

Carrie frowned and bit her lip. "I—well, I *could* probably be a better catcher if I didn't let go of the ball too soon."

"I would love to help you with that," Mary smiled. "Now, would you mind weeding the garden while I lie down?"

As Diana and Carrie worked in the garden, a funny look passed over Carrie's face. "You don't think plants have feelings, do you?"

Diana looked at her friend. "NO!"